Max Spaniel
Dinosaur Hunt

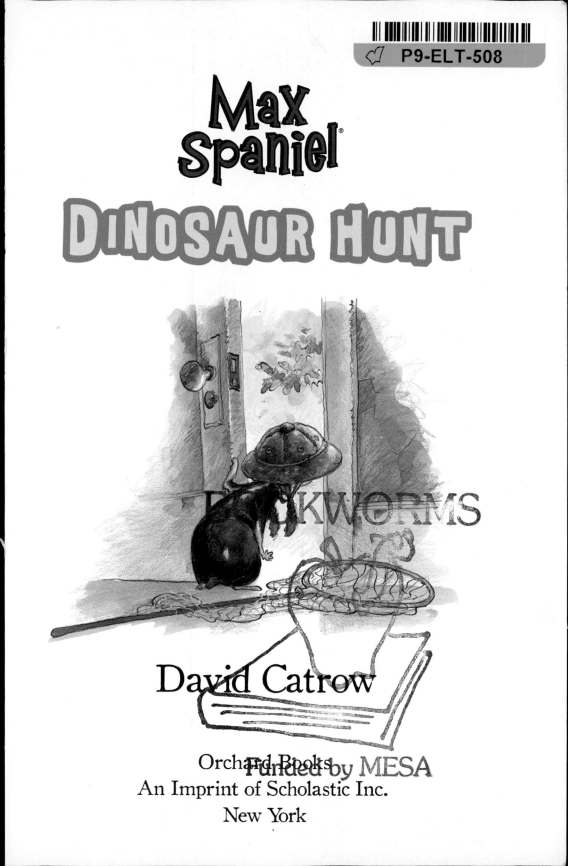

David Catrow

Orchard Books
An Imprint of Scholastic Inc.
New York

For Bubbs, Beetle, and Blu

All rights reserved. Published by Orchard Books, an imprint of Scholastic Inc.,
Publishers since 1920. ORCHARD BOOKS and design are registered trademarks of Watts
Publishing Group, Ltd., used under license. SCHOLASTIC and associated logos are
trademarks and/or registered trademarks of Scholastic Inc.

Library of Congress Cataloging-in-Publication Data is available.

ISBN 978-0-545-05751-6

10 9 8 7 6 5 4 3 2   10   11   12   13   14   15

Printed in the U.S.A. 40
This edition first printing, September 2010

My name is Max.
I am not a dog.

I am a great hunter.

I love to hunt dinosaurs.
I hunt with my ears.

I hunt with
my eyes.

I hunt with my nose.

No dinosaurs.

I have an idea.
I will go outside.

What can I take?

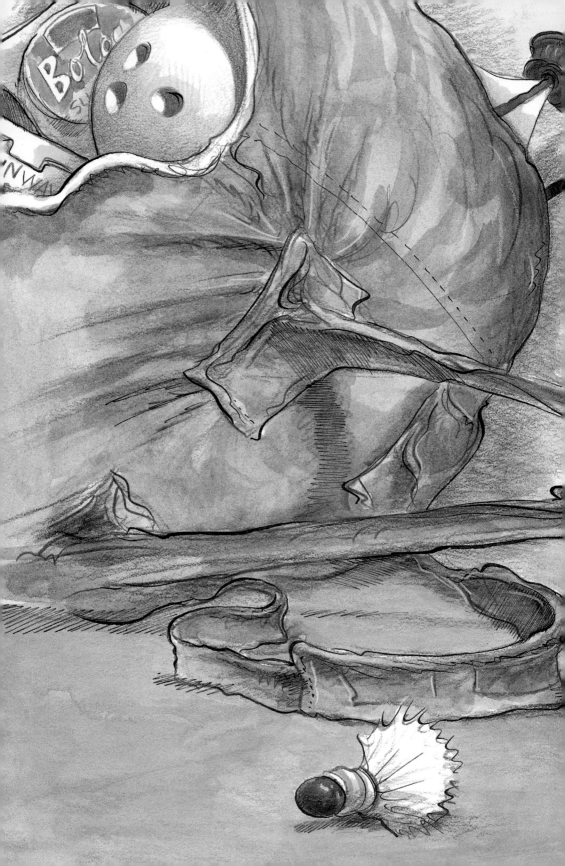

This is too much.

I take what I need.

I don't give up.

What is this?
It's a dinosaur bone!

A great hunter knows where to look.

I spy an eye.

I see a head in the flower bed.

I see a rib.

I see a knee.

Here is a neck.

Here are hips.

Here are two lips.

Teeth help him tear and rip.

Here is a claw.

Here is a jaw.

Here is a toenail.

Here is a long
green tail.

Part by part,
step by step,
the dinosaur stands.

Part by part,
step by step,
the dinosaur comes alive.

He walks again.